Dogbird

and other
mixed-up tales

Paul Stewart

Illustrated by Tony Ross

DOGBIRD AND OTHER MIXED-UP TALES
A CORGI PUPS BOOK 9780552553513

This collection first published in Great Britain by Corgi Pups,
an imprint of Random House Children's Books

This edition published 2006

3 5 7 9 10 8 6 4 2

MIX
Paper from
responsible sources
FSC
www.fsc.org **FSC® C018072**

Set in 18/25 Bembo MT Schoolbook

Corgi Pups are published by Random House Children's Books,
61–63 Uxbridge Road, London W5 5SA,
A Random House Group Company

A C[...]   [...].
The Rar   [...]dship
Council® ([...]isation.
Our bool   [...]paper.
FSC is   [...]ding
       e[...]

Pr[...]   c

Contents

Contents

Dogbird

Chapter One

It was lunchtime. Alice Carey was sitting at the table with her mum and dad. The radio was on, but the music was drowned out by the sound of howling.

"That wretched bird is driving me round the bend!" Dad muttered.

At that moment the door burst open, and Lex, Lol and Lance – the family's three black labradors – bounded into the room and barked up at the birdcage.

Alice's mum jumped up. As she did so, the table-cloth got caught round her leg, and the whole lot – plates of lasagne, glasses of water and orange squash, knives and forks, salt and pepper – came crashing to the floor.

"That's it!" her dad stormed.
"That bird has got to go!"

* * *

The bird in question was a budgie. He belonged to Alice.

On her seventh birthday, her mum and dad had taken her to the pet-shop to choose her very own pet. But what animal would be best?

With Lex, Lol and Lance
around, it wouldn't be fair to
buy a kitten.

And Alice thought that guinea
pigs were boring.

And Alice's mum refused to
have a snake in the house!

So it was that, after much
humming and haaing, Alice
chose a budgie.

"Perfect," said Mum.

"Ideal," said Dad.

It was only later that they
discovered how wrong they had
both been.

The pet-shop man told them
the budgie was a talker. On the
way home, Alice sat in the car
with the cage on her lap. She
tried to teach him a couple of
things. *"Who's a clever boy,
then?"* and *"My name's Blue."*

But by the time they pulled
up outside Alice's house, the
budgie hadn't said a single word.

"Wait till we get him inside,"
said Mum. "He'll soon find his
voice then."

Mum turned the key in the
lock and pushed the door open.
Lex, Lol and Lance raced into
the hallway. Normally, they
were quiet, but the sight and
smell of the bright blue bird
seemed to drive them crazy.

Time and again they jumped up at the cage, barking furiously.

And the budgie? Well, Alice's mum was right. He did find his voice. He opened his beak and barked back at them.

"Dogbird," Dad laughed –
and the name stuck.

From that moment on, life in
the Carey family changed – and
for the worse. For although it
seemed funny at first, a barking
budgie was no joke.

Dogbird barked at the milkman.
He barked at the postman.

He barked when Alice's friends
came to play. And every time
he barked, Lex, Lol and Lance
would join in. It drove everyone
bonkers.

Woof! Woof! Woof!

Louder and louder, they
would get. The budgie and the
dogs, all barking wildly together.
Once they'd started nothing
would make them stop.

Woof! Woof! Woof!

Sometimes the dogs would escape from the kitchen into the sitting-room where Dogbird's cage hung by the window. It was then that the barking grew loudest of all. You couldn't hear yourself think.

WOOF! WOOF! WOOF! WOOF!

Day after day, the barking would start up. Night after night, everyone's sleep was disturbed. The neighbours complained. Someone wrote to the council.

Now, six weeks later, with the
dogs jumping around in the
remains of their lunch and
Dogbird still loudly barking,
Alice's dad had finally reached
the end of his tether.

Chapter Two

Before Alice could protest, the
telephone rang. It was Grandma
and, from the look on her mum's
face, something was wrong.

"Oh, how awful," she said.
"Stay where you are. We'll be
right over." She put the phone
down. "Grandma's been
burgled."

Alice shuddered. "Poor
Grandma," she said. "She'll
want one of my special
cuddles."

"No, Alice. Not now," said
her mum. "Grandma sounded in
rather a state. You can play
with Katie while we go and see
how she is."

"We'll be seeing her again
tomorrow," said Dad. "You can
cuddle her then."

Alice knew there was no point arguing – at least they'd forgotten about Dogbird. At that moment, though, Lex, Lol and Lance came tearing back into the room to remind them. Their wagging tails sent everything flying. The barking was deafening!

"Not again!" Mum shouted.
"Get to your baskets, the lot of
you!"

"I'll tell you what," said Dad,
as he grabbed the dogs by their
collars. "*We'd* never get burgled.
A loud dog is better than any
alarm."

"And we've got three!" said
Mum.

Dogbird growled. Alice stared
at him sadly.

"Four," she said quietly.

Katie was Alice's best friend and
next-door neighbour. As they sat
together in Katie's tree-house,
Alice told her all about the
burglars.

"They took *everything!*" she
said.

"Everything?" gasped Katie.

"All Grandma's secret treasures," Alice said. She was enjoying the look of wide-eyed horror on her friend's face. "Of course," she said, "*we'd* never get burgled – because of the dogs."

Katie nodded. "I wish we had a dog," she said. "Dad says

they're too much trouble. And too noisy."

"But it's the noise that's important," said Alice. "The barking frightens the burglars away..."

As she spoke, the noise in question – barking – exploded from Alice's house. It was Lex, Lol, Lance and, loudest of all, Dogbird.

Katie spun round. "Burglars!" she cried.

But Alice didn't think so.
"Quick!" she cried. "Before
we're too late!"

Chapter Three

The two girls leapt down from
the tree-house, slipped through
the hole in the fence, and raced
to the back of Alice's house.

They peered in through the
window. Alice saw the dogs
leaping about, the cage on its
side – the flapping wings.

"DOGBIRD!" she screamed.

She hammered on the glass,
but the dogs took no notice.
Their game was far too much
fun.

Alice dashed to the back door,
through the kitchen and into the
sitting-room. When she got
there, things had gone from bad
to worse.

The cage door had sprung
open and Dogbird was now
free. He was fluttering between

the lights and the picture-rail,
with the dogs crashing about
after him.

They knocked over the coffee
table, they leapt on the settee,
they scrabbled up the wall
shelves. Books tumbled, cushions
flew. There was millet everywhere.

Crash!

Mum's favourite vase lay in pieces on the floor.

"GET TO YOUR BASKETS," Alice bellowed.

The dogs froze. The game was clearly over. Heads down and tails between their legs, they plodded back to the kitchen.

Alice slammed the door behind
them and hurried to Dogbird.

Katie had stood the cage up,
and Dogbird was back inside,
trembling.

"Poor thing," said Alice. "Did
the naughty doggies frighten
you?" She turned to Katie. "It's
been like this ever since I got
him."

"I know," said Katie. "I live next door, remember."

"Is it *really* noisy?" Alice asked.

"Sometimes," said Katie. "It makes Dad so grumpy."

"I'm sorry," said Alice.
"It's the dogs – they won't leave
him alone."

Katie shrugged. "Perhaps it's
not their fault."

"What do you mean?" said
Alice.

"Well," she said. "What do you think a dog says when it barks?"

Alice laughed. "*Hello*, I suppose."

"Or, *Go away! I'm dangerous!*" said Katie.

"Or, *Let's play!*" said Alice.

"Exactly!" said Katie.
"And those are the things that
Dogbird is saying to them when
he barks. The dogs are only
responding. They're probably
just trying to get him out of the
cage so they can go and play."

Alice nodded. It made sense.
Trust her to end up with a
budgie that could only speak
dog.

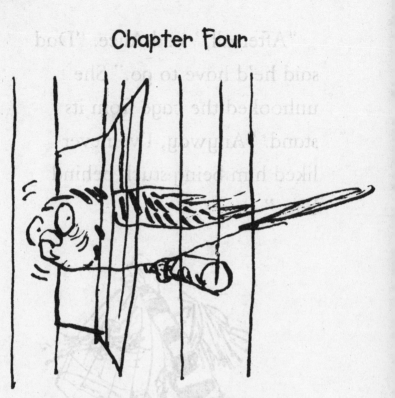

Chapter Four

Afterwards, neither Alice nor
Katie could remember who first
suggested setting Dogbird free.
The idea just sort of happened,
the way ideas sometimes do.

"After all," said Alice, "Dad said he'd have to go." She unhooked the cage from its stand. "Anyway, I've never liked him being stuck behind bars."

"He must get lonely on his own," said Katie. She followed her friend across the room. "In Australia, the wild ones live in flocks."

Alice sighed. "All Dogbird's
got is his reflection."

She opened the French
windows and stepped outside.
Dogbird wagged his tail
feathers.

"He can hear the call of the
wild," Katie whispered.

"A bird needs to be free," said
Alice. She opened the cage door.
Dogbird didn't move. "I said ...
Dogbird! Get out of there."

47

Dogbird hopped to the end of the perch, and watched Alice through one mistrustful eye. Alice reached inside the cage. Dogbird growled and snapped at her fingers.

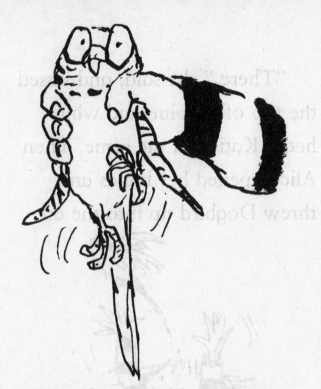

But Alice would not be put
off. She had decided to set
Dogbird free, and that was what
she was going to do. Quickly
and gently, she closed her hand
around his body, and pulled him
from the cage.

"There," she said, and kissed the top of his blue and white head. Katie did the same. Then Alice opened her hands and threw Dogbird up into the air.

"*Woof!*" said Dogbird, and soared off into the sunset – a flash of sky-blue.

"He did it!" Katie shouted
excitedly.

Alice nodded. There was a
lump in her throat. "Bye-bye,
Dogbird," she whispered. "Be
happy!"

They were stepping back into
the house when a sudden noise

filled the air. Horrible it was! A stomach-churning screeching and squawking and jabbering – and above it all, the sound of frenzied barking.

"Look!" Katie cried, but Alice had already seen.

High above the treetops, Dogbird was being attacked. There were sparrows, starlings, blackbirds, magpies, crows – all ganging up on the sky-blue intruder.

"Leave him alone!" Alice
screamed.

But it was no good. The birds
wouldn't rest until they had
driven Dogbird away. Or worse!

"It's all gone wrong," Alice
wailed, as Dogbird darted this
way and that, trying to avoid
the sharp beaks and claws.

"Dogbird!" she called. "Come back!"

As if only waiting to be asked, Dogbird barked, twisted round in mid-air and swooped down towards her. The flock of furious birds followed close behind.

"Faster," yelled Katie.

Alice stretched out her arm.
Dogbird flew closer, barking all
the while – and landed. The
other birds flew off and
chattered angrily from the tree
and fence. Dogbird shivered
miserably. There were spots of
blood on his wing.

"Now what?" said Alice
sadly. She hung the cage back
on its stand.

Katie shrugged.
Dogbird barked.
And both girls
heard the sound of
the key in the lock.

"Hello?" said Dad, surprised.
"What are you two doing
here?"

"And what's all this mess?"
Mum demanded.

"It was the dogs," Alice
explained. "They knocked the
bird-cage over." Dad groaned.

Then, not wanting to tell them about trying to set Dogbird free, she asked, "How's Grandma?"

"Fine," said Mum. "But a bit worried the burglars might come back."

"She should get a dog," said Dad. "She'd feel much safer."

"She couldn't cope," said Mum. "The walks, the feeds ..."

Alice and Katie looked at one another and grinned. That was it! That was the answer.

"What if I gave her Dogbird?" said Alice.

Mum smiled. "Perfect!" she said.

"Ideal!" said Dad.

And this time, they were right.

★ ★ ★

And so it was that Dogbird went to live with Grandma. Life in the Carey household changed again – this time for the better.

The dogs stopped barking.

The neighbours stopped complaining. And everyone finally got a good night's sleep.

As for Grandma, she was overjoyed with the budgie. He kept her company and was no trouble at all. She called him Bluey.

Alice often went to see the
pair of them. She was pleased to
see that the bird was happy at
last. Grandma kept the cage
door open so that Bluey could
fly in and out as he pleased. He
never tried to escape – even
when the windows were open.

And being with Grandma, he
soon learned to speak.

"*Pretty Bluey*," he would say.
And sometimes, "*Now where
have I put my glasses?*"

Best of all, he made Grandma
feel safe. Whenever the gate
clicked, or the doorbell rang, or
he heard someone prowling
around outside, Bluey would
become Dogbird again, and
bark and bark and bark.

The Were-Pig

Chapter One

"You did *what*?" exclaimed Nan Tucker.

"I took a Mars bar from Joanne's lunch-box," said Albert.

"And did you eat it?"

Albert blushed and looked down at the floor.

"Well?" she said.

Albert nodded. "Yes," he admitted.

Nan Tucker breathed in noisily. "But this is serious," she said. "Very serious."

Albert Amis was nine. Two years earlier his parents had split up, and his dad left home for good.

Mum had tried to cope on her own, but it wasn't easy. She had to leave for work at seven in the morning, and never got home before seven in the evening.

When the summer holidays came around, the situation became impossible. That was when Nan Tucker moved in with them.

Nan Tucker was Albert's mum's mum. Tall and skinny, with bright red hair and dark green eyes, she wasn't like any other grandmothers that Albert knew. None of *them* wore long patchwork skirts or had beads plaited into their hair.

But Albert wouldn't have had Nan Tucker any other way. She was fun. She played the guitar, and told brilliant stories. She took him on long walks – and never minded him keeping the things his mum would have made him leave behind, like owl-pellets and beetles and the skeletons of small animals and birds. She showed him how to make things, too — a robot, a radio and chocolate chip cookies.

And when Albert had
wanted a pet, it
was Nan Tucker
who persuaded
his mum to let
him have the
white rat he'd
set his heart
on.

All in all,
Nan Tucker was the perfect
grandmother – which was why
her reaction to the Mars bar
was so worrying. If Nan Tucker
said it was serious, then Albert
knew it really was serious.

"But it's not fair!" he said.
"Joanne had a Mars bar, a Kit-
Kat *and* a bag of wine gums. All
I had was one of those boring
muesli chews – and I hate
them."

"Then you should have told me," said Nan Tucker. "Anything, rather than letting your greed get the better of you."

Albert winced. He could still see the Mars bar nestled up in the corner of Joanne's lunchbox, and Joanne herself, busy talking to Ella. He'd slipped his

hand inside the lunch-box,
shoved the chocolate bar up his
sleeve and left before Joanne
noticed it was missing. Then,
outside on the school field, he'd
pulled off the wrapper and
eaten it all in one go. It had
tasted delicious.

"One last question," said Nan Tucker. "Was the sun shining?"

Albert thought back. "Yes," he said.

"Oh, dear," said Nan Tucker. "Oh, dearie-dear! Such a display of greed, and by the light of the full-sun! Do you know what this means, Albert?"

Albert shook his head. "What?" he said.

"Unless I'm very much mistaken – and I seldom am," she added, "you have brought upon yourself the curse of the were-pig!"

Chapter Two

"Were-pig?" said Albert alarmed. "I've heard of a were-*wolf*, but . . ."

"Were-wolf? *Pah!*" said Nan Tucker. "There's no such thing.

All that howling at the full-
moon nonsense! A were-*pig*, on
the other hand, is all too real."

"But what is it?" asked Albert.

"A greedy monster," came the hushed reply. "Half-human, half pig. It emerges when the sun is full . . ."

"This is just one of your stories, right?" said Albert, laughing uneasily. "I mean,  for a start, the sun is always full."

"Precisely," said Nan Tucker darkly.

"I . . . I don't understand," said Albert.

"Greed drove you to take that Mars bar in broad daylight," said Nan Tucker. "Now, whenever the sun appears from behind the clouds, that same greed will change you into a were-pig. Snout, trotters, curly tail – the whole caboodle."

"No," Albert gasped. "It can't
be true."

"Oh, but it can," said Nan Tucker. "If it wasn't dark outside now, you'd see."

"But how long will it last?" said Albert. "A day? A month? For ever?"

Nan Tucker shrugged. "That, I cannot say."

Albert found it hard to go to sleep
that night. Of course, he knew
Nan Tucker was only joking –

she'd just been trying to frighten
him so that he'd never take anything from anyone again. There
was no such thing as a were-
pig. How could there be?

And yet . . .

What if there was? What if he
really did turn into a were-pig?
What *then*?

The next morning, Albert woke
early. He jumped out of bed,
ran to the window and peeked
out through the curtains.

Heavy rain was falling from a
dark, cloudy sky.

"Thank goodness for that!"
he said.

After breakfast, Albert put on
his shoes and waterproof. Nan
Tucker handed him his lunch-
box at the door.

"I put a Mars bar in," she
said, and winked. "Have a lovely
day, Albert."

"I will," said Albert. He was
pleased she hadn't mentioned
the business of the were-pig. It
must have been a joke.

Joke or no joke, Albert couldn't stop thinking about the curse of the were-pig. All through numeracy-hour he kept checking to see that it hadn't stopped raining.

"Albert!" Mrs Wilkinson
snapped at last. "If I catch you
looking out of the window once
more, I'll keep you in at break."

"Sorry, Mrs Wilkinson," said
Albert. "It won't happen again."

But it did.

At a quarter to ten, the rain had turned to light drizzle. At ten o'clock it had stopped completely. And at a quarter past, Albert was dismayed to see

the sun glowing brightly behind the thinning clouds. Uh-oh, he thought.

"That's it, Albert!" Mrs Wilkinson shouted. "You will not go out to play." Ten minutes later, the bell went. While all the other children streamed out of the class and into the playground, followed by Mrs Wilkinson, Albert stayed in his seat.

And there he remained, tired after his broken night's sleep, while outside, the hidden sun grew warmer and brighter.

He laid his head on his elbow and stared miserably out of the window through half-closed eyes. Any moment now, the sun would burst through the clouds. Any moment . . .

Chapter Three

"Aargh!" Albert shrieked, as dazzling beams of sunlight streamed down from the sky. 'Aaar . . . *weeeiiiii!*"

Albert fell still, horrified by

the noise he had just made. It
had definitely been a squeal. His
hand shot up to his mouth.

"Oink!" he grunted in horror
as his fingers touched, not his
mouth, but a snout.

"Oink!" he grunted again as his
hands twisted and hardened, to
form two trotters.

He reached round anxiously –
and there it was: a
short, curly tail
sticking out from a
hole in his trouser.
"OI-INK!"

It had happened! Albert had changed into a were-pig.

What was worse, the terrible transformation had left him feeling hungrier than he'd ever felt before. He had to eat something; anything – *everything!* Now!

As he headed for the door, Albert found that walking on two legs was too

difficult with all the extra
weight he had to carry. With a
sigh, he dropped down onto all
fours. Along the corridor he
scurried, round a corner, past
reception and into the
dining-hall – drawn on by
the snout-watering smells
wafting from the kitchen.

The dinner-ladies were setting up the tables and chairs. They didn't see Albert darting across the floor.

So far, so good, he thought as, head down, he charged at the swing doors. With a thud, they burst open. Albert ran inside and squealed with delight.

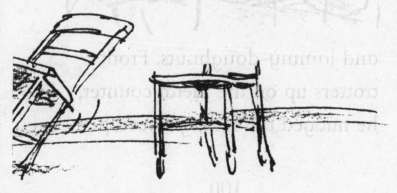

Food! He was surrounded
by food!

First off, Albert made for
the warming-cabinet. Inside it
were pies and pasties, hot-dogs
and burgers, apple turnovers

and jammy-doughnuts. Front
trotters up on the metal counter,
he nudged the sliding-door open

with his snout, thrust his head
inside and began gorging
himself.

Sweet or savoury, it didn't
matter. The air was soon filled
with splattered jam and gravy,
and a flurry of flaky pastry.

Within minutes every last morsel
was gone – and Albert was
hungrier than ever.

He heaved himself up onto the
serving-counter and waddled
along the row of steel containers.
Each one held something more
delicious than the last.

Hotpot . . .
Baked beans . . .
Chips . . .

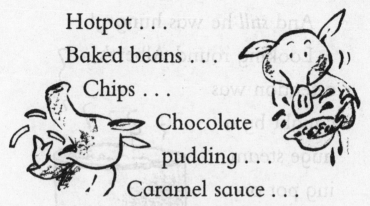

Chocolate
pudding . . .
Caramel sauce . . .
Albert plunged his head into
every single one of them, and
guzzled down the food in great,
greedy mouthfuls.

And *still* he was hungry!

Looking round, Albert's attention was caught by a huge steam-ing pot on the stove. He sniffed – once,

twice – and a smile spread over his piggy features. It was his favourite. Custard.

Albert took a flying leap
through the air – forgetting
for a moment that pigs *can't* fly

– and careered into the great
pot of custard. The pot toppled
backwards and fell to the floor
with a loud *crash*! The custard
went everywhere.

But Albert didn't care. He dropped down after it, pushed his snout into the sweet, yellow goo, and began slurping noisily.

Unfortunately, the dinner-
ladies had also heard the crash.

"What was that?"
shouted one.

"I'll check!"
shouted another.

Grunting with
frustration, Albert abandoned the
delicious custard. He trotted off
and hid himself under the sink.

"What on earth . . . !" he
heard the dinner-lady exclaim.
"Madge! Vera! Come and look
at this!"

Albert kept as quiet as he could. He didn't want to be spotted — and if it hadn't been for the slop-bucket,
he might not have been. But the delicious smell of the potato-peel and carrot-
tops and pea-pods proved irresistible to Albert.

He leaned forwards. He pushed his head deep down into the bucket — and got it stuck fast.

Chapter Four

No matter how hard Albert shook his head, or tried to prise the bucket off with his trotters, he could not free himself. The bucket would not budge. What

was worse, the shrieking of the
dinner-ladies was coming closer.

"I've got to get
out of here," Albert
snorted. "And quick!"

He jumped up
and dashed across the
kitchen. With the bucket over his
head, he couldn't see a thing.

He blundered
around
noisily,
desperately
trying to
find a way
out.

"It's a pig!" the dinner-ladies were screaming. "And it's been at the food!"

Albert felt two rough hands grasp his curly tail.

Squealing with indignation, he pulled away, skidded off over the slippery floor and . . .

THUD!

For a moment, Albert thought he'd hit the wall. But no. At last, he'd had some good luck. He'd found the swing-doors and was back inside the dining-hall.

As he tried to cross the floor,
Albert soon discovered that the
dining-hall was an even worse
place to be than the kitchen.
Whichever way he turned he
knocked into things.

Bang! Clatter! CRASH!
Leaving behind him a tangled
mass of tables and chairs, Albert
ran blindly down a corridor.

Then another. And another. He
didn't know where he was now.
Everywhere seemed the same.

Finally, Albert gave up. He sat
down heavily on
the floor and
closed his eyes.
He had no
choice but to
wait for some-
one to come
and help him.

"Oink," he grunted sadly.
Now everyone would discover
his terrible secret. "Oink!"

"Albert Amis!" came an angry
voice. "Is
that you?"

Albert froze. It was Mrs
Wilkinson. He felt two hands
seize the bucket and pull it off
his head.

"What on earth are you
doing sitting on the floor with
the waste-paper bin on your
head?" she said.

"I . . . I . . ." Albert
stammered. He reached up
nervously and touched . . . his
mouth. And with fingers, not
trotters. He felt round for the
curly tail, but that too had gone.

"Clowning about," said Mrs Wilkinson, answering her own question. "And I'll have no more of it. Do you understand?"

"Yes, Mrs Wilkinson. Sorry, Mrs Wilkinson," he said.

He was a boy again, not a were-pig – even with the full-sun streaming in through the windows of his classroom.

The bell rang, and the rest of
the class began filing back to their
tables.

"And from now on," said
Albert, "I promise I'll be good."
And this time, he was.

★

"How was school today?" Nan Tucker called when she heard the front-door closing.

"Fine," said Albert. He'd decided to keep quiet about the were-pig incident. She'd only worry. "Except for one thing."

Nan Tucker
appeared from the
kitchen, drying
her hands on
a tea-towel.
"What was
that?" she
said.

"The Mars
bar you said you put in my
lunch-box," said
Albert. "When
I went to
eat it, it
wasn't
there."

"Wasn't there?" said Nan Tucker, her eyes gleaming mischievously. "Do you think someone could have taken it?"

Albert shook his head. "Perhaps," he said.

"Well, more fool them if they have," said Nan Tucker. "They'll have brought the curse of the were-pig down on themselves.

And if the curse is on *them* then it's no longer on *you*!" She frowned. "But be careful, Albert. Next time you might not be so lucky."

"Next time?" said Albert. "There's not going to be a next time. Ever."

Nan Tucker smiled. "Good," she said. "That's *just* what I wanted to hear!'

THE END

The
Watch-Frog

Chapter One

"Go away!" Looby shouted
down from her bedroom window.
"Go on. Hop it!"

The frog took no notice.

"*Ribbit!*" it went. "*Ribbit!*"

Looby slammed the window shut, climbed back into bed and wrapped her pillow round her head. But she could still hear the frog croaking loudly in the garden pond.

"Ribbit! Ribbit! Ribbit!"

Louise Mitchell – or Looby, as
everyone knew her – was eight
years old. She lived with her
mum and dad in a tall, thin
terraced house. Looby had the
back bedroom, where it was
supposed to be quiet.

It had been – until the frog arrived.

Now, each morning at four o'clock on the dot, the frog would start croaking. It was still croaking when she went to bed in the evening. The awful noise had been going on for five days.

Looby was fed up – and very, very tired.

Every Friday afternoon Looby's grandfather would pick her up from school. Usually he would greet her with, "Looby! My favourite granddaughter!" – which was a sort of joke, since she was his *only* granddaughter.

On this particular Friday, however – a week after the arrival of the infuriating frog – Grandad's first words were quite different.

"Looby!" he said. "There are deep, dark circles under your eyes. What have you been doing? You look *so* tired."

"I am," Looby admitted, and yawned. "Exhausted!"

"Let's get home," said Grandad, "and you can tell me all about it. I've got us a special treat this afternoon," he added. "Jam doughnuts!"

"Oh, Looby!" Grandad laughed, when Looby had finished telling him all about the frog. "Is that all?"

"But you don't understand," said Looby. "It's deafening."

"Frogs *can* be loud in May and June," Grandad nodded. "Especially the males. He's calling for a mate." He frowned thoughtfully and rubbed his chin. "Un-less . . ." he said slowly.

Looby looked at him. "Unless what?"

Grandad sat down and drew
his chair closer. "Unless it's not a
frog at all," he said.

"Not a frog?" said Looby. "Of
course it's a frog. I've seen it."

"Oh, I'm sure it *looks* like a
frog," said Grandad. "But why
should it be croaking during
the day? That's very unusual."

He drew closer. His voice turned to a hushed whisper. "What if it's a person who's been turned into a frog by a wicked witch? You remember the story of the Frog Prince . . ."

"Oh, Grandad," said Looby, disappointed. "I'm too old for fairy tales about wicked witches and magic spells."

Grandad leaned back. "Perhaps you are," he said. "But just because you no longer believe in magic, it doesn't mean it no longer exists." And he pulled a shiny coin from her ear.

Looby laughed. Then, remembering what the princess in the fairy tale had done, she said, "And I'll tell you this, Grandad. Magic or no magic, I do *not* intend to kiss it. Ever!"

Grandad smiled mysteriously. "We'll see," he said.

Chapter Two

Dear old Grandad, thought
Looby as she walked home.

To him, she was still the same
wide-eyed little girl who had
been enchanted by his magical
tales. But Looby was big now.

She knew the frog in her garden
was just that – a frog. And a
horribly loud one at that.

On Saturday morning when
the frog woke her – at four
o'clock on the dot! – Looby
decided to take action.

Ribbit
Ribbit
Ribbit

She went downstairs, out of the
back door and into the garden.
The frog was on a lily-pad in
the middle of the pond, croaking
for all it was worth.

"*Ribbit! Rib*—"

"I'll teach you to wake me up so early!" Looby cried as she seized it in her hand. She stomped across the lawn to the back fence and tossed it into the stream which ran behind the row of gardens.

Ribb

"*Ribbit!*" said the frog.

"Just go away!" Looby
shouted and marched back to
the house – and her warm, cosy,
and finally *quiet* bed.

It didn't stay quiet for
long. By six o'clock
the frog was back
and croaking louder
than ever.

Ribbit Ribbit Ribbit

"That's it!" Looby said. She
got dressed and went
down to the
kitchen.

"You're up early," said Mum.
"Did that frog wake you up
again?"

"Yes, it did!" said Looby
crossly. "Twice! And I'm going
to make sure it never does
again."

"Oh, Looby," said Mum, "I hope you're not going to hurt it."

"Of course I'm not," she said. "But I'm going to catch it and then we're going to take it a long, long way away . . ."

Looby had decided to release the frog at Lidden Lake, a beauty spot about half a mile away. With the frog inside a plastic sandwich-box, she and her mum climbed into the car and set off. Five minutes later they were standing at the water's edge.

"Would you like some bread
for the ducks?" Mum asked.

"First things first," said Looby.
She opened the lid of the
sandwich-box and tipped it up.

The frog plopped down into the water. "Bye-bye, froggy," said Looby as the frog kicked its legs and disappeared. "And good riddance!"

That evening Looby lay in
bed listening to the quiet. "At
last!" she muttered happily. And
she rolled over and fell into a
deep, deep sleep.

Chapter Three

"*Ribbit! Ribbit!*"

Looby's eyes snapped open.
She looked at the clock. It was
four o'clock – and the frog was
back!

But how had it returned from so far away? And so quickly? And how had it found its way? And, most important of all, *why?*

"*Ribbit! Ribbit!*"

Was it a super-frog? Looby wondered. Or might Grandad have been right all along?

"*Ribbit! Ribbit!*"

"Don't be ridiculous!" Looby told herself. "Spawn, tadpole, frog – that's the way it happens. But human being to frog . . ." She shook her head. "It's impossible."

"*Ribbit! Rib—*"
The frog abruptly stopped croaking. The silence that followed seemed to echo round the room.

Looby ran to the window.
And there, next to the pond, was
Pugsy – next door's big ginger
tom – with two froggy legs
sticking out of his mouth.

For a moment Looby
considered doing nothing about
it. But only for a moment. No
frog – however noisy – deserved
to be eaten by Pugsy.

She tore downstairs and into
the garden. "Pugsy!" she shouted.
"Put it down!"

The cat purred. The frog
kicked its legs weakly.

"PUGSY!"

Looby grabbed him by the scruff of his neck and eased his jaws open. The frog tumbled to the ground, where it lay still. There was blood on one of its front legs.

"Pugsy, you naughty cat!" said
Looby, and shooed him away.

Then she picked up the limp,
trembling creature. "Oh, froggy,"
she said, "I never wanted *this* to
happen. You poor little thing."

And before Looby knew quite what she was doing, she had put the frog to her puckered lips and planted a tiny kiss right on the end of its mouth.

"Thank you," the frog croaked weakly.

Looby started back in surprise. "I ... I ... I ..." she stammered.

"But please put
me down," the
frog continued.
"Your hands
are unpleasantly
warm."

Looby did as she was told.
The kiss hadn't turned the frog
into a handsome prince – but it
had made it speak.

"H-have you
had a magic
spell put on
you?" she asked.

The frog
nodded.

"By a wicked witch?" said Looby.

"The wickedest!" said the frog.

"But . . . this is just what my grandad told me," said Looby.

"Then your grandad is a wise man," said the frog. "Not many people believe in such things nowadays. *I* didn't . . ." it added, with a long, sorrowful sigh.

"But what happened?" said Looby.

"It's a long story," said the frog.

"Let me get this straight," said Looby, when the frog had

finished. "You're not a frog at all, you're a twelve-year-old boy who was at a seaside adventure camp."

"You've got it," said the frog. "My parents send me there every year while they're off trekking up the Amazon."

"And last Sunday, while you were diving off the coast, you bumped into a witch."

"A *water*-witch," the frog corrected her.

"And *she* turned you into a frog."

"Yes," said the frog, and shuddered. "I can still see her long sharp nails and horrible bloodshot eyes. And that voice!

I'll teach you to come poking your nose into every whelk and barnacle, and scaring the fish, she screeched."

"She sounds awful," gasped Looby.

"She was!" said the frog. "*And since you're so keen on watching others, Mr Froggy-man, she went on, that's exactly what you shall be. A watch-frog! And so you shall remain until the time when you help someone out!* Then she cackled with laughter, snapped her

fingers and – *kazam!* – I was
here, as you see me now. I
think I'm meant to be *your*
watch-frog."

"Just my luck," said Looby. "I haven't slept properly for a week."

"Yes, I'm sorry about that," said the frog. "I was just trying to get your attention."

Looby nodded. "I suppose I'd have done exactly the same thing," she said, then added, "But won't anyone be missing you?"

 The frog shook its
head. "It's all
been a bit of a
mix-up," it
explained. "My
parents think I'm at the camp.
The camp thinks my parents
came to pick me up. Somehow,
I've got to turn
back into my real
self before they
get back and
find me gone."

"And when's
that?" Looby
asked.

"In eight days," said the frog.

"So, before they do," said Looby, remembering the water-witch's words, "you've got to help me out."

"Exactly," said the frog. "And that's not easy when

you're small, squidgy and only
eight centimetres long. I haven't
a clue what to do."

"Me neither," Looby admitted.
"But one thing's certain," she
said as she noticed Pugsy sitting
on the fence, licking his lips.

"You can't stay out here. There's
an old aquarium in the lean-to.
I'll get some gravel and pond-
weed, and put you in that."

"Thank you," said the frog
for a second time.

By the time Looby had found
the aquarium and washed it
out, she was beginning to yawn.
It was, after all, still only five
o'clock in the morning.

"Leave the gravel and pond-weed for now," said the frog. "Get some more sleep. You look shattered!"

"And whose fault is that?" said Looby crossly.

"I told you I was sorry," said the frog. "I'll be quiet from now on, I promise."

Chapter Four

Looby slept till ten o'clock that Sunday morning, when her mum woke her up with a cup of tea. "It's a lovely day," she said, "You don't want to waste it all." She smiled. "Though I'm glad you got a good night's sleep for once."

"So am I, Mum," said Looby.
"Oh, but I had the weirdest
dream. All about a talking
frog . . ."

"That reminds me," said her
mum. "What are you planning
to do with that frog in the
aquarium?"

"Frog?"
Looby
spluttered.
"Aquarium?
It can't be . . ."

She leaped out of bed and
raced downstairs. And sure
enough, there in the lean-to

where she hoped she'd only *dreamed* she'd left it, was the frog.

Looby's head spun. Was she going crazy? Since the frog was in the aquarium, it couldn't have been a dream. But if it *wasn't* a dream . . .

She picked up the frog. "Can you speak?" she said.

The frog remained silent.

"Well, *can* you?" she said. "I didn't even ask your name."

Still nothing. Not a word – not even a croaky little *ribbit*.

Looby didn't know what to think, but with Pugsy still on the prowl, she couldn't return the frog to the pond. So she equipped its new home with the

gravel and pond-weed, and
brought it slugs, bugs and worms
to eat. Then she carried the
whole lot up to her bedroom
and placed it on her desk.

"But you'd better remember
your promise!" she said.

The frog did remember. The days
passed, and not once did it wake
her up or stop her going to sleep.

"The mating season's over," Grandad explained that Friday. "That's why it's so quiet."

But Looby was not so sure. She couldn't forget her dream – if it *was* a dream.

Whatever the reason, the frog was quiet now – and so it might have stayed if it hadn't been for Dad's little accident.

"RIBBIT! RIBBIT!"
Looby sat bolt upright in bed.

It was pitch-black
outside. She looked at
her clock. "Twenty to
one!" she groaned.

"*RIBBIT! RIBBIT!*"

"What's the matter?" said
Looby.

The frog jumped up and down
in the aquarium. "*RIBBIT!*" it
cried. "**RIBBIT!!**"

And then Looby smelt it . . .
Gas!

"MUM! DAD!" she bellowed.
"I CAN SMELL GAS!"

Two fire engines, an ambulance
and a man from the gas board
arrived minutes after Mum's 999
call.

It didn't take them long to
find the leak. Looby's dad was
called back into the house.

"Someone been doing a spot of DIY, have they?" said the chief fire-fighter.

"This is highly irregular," said the man from the gas board. "Boilers must only be installed by qualified fitters."

"I know . . . I thought . . . That is, I didn't . . ." Dad muttered.

"Everything's safe now, sir," said the chief fire-fighter. "Just remember, some jobs are best left to professionals."
When the fire-fighters, ambulance crew and the man from the gas board had finally all gone, Looby's mum turned to her. "Oh, Looby," she said. "Thank heavens you woke up when you did."

"It was the frog," said Looby.

"The *watch-frog* . . ."

Suddenly, the frog's words came back to her. She charged back up to her bedroom. The aquarium was empty. The frog was nowhere to be seen. Then she noticed them . . .

Footprints.
Big, wet footprints.

Big, wet, *flipper*-shaped footprints crossing the carpet from the desk to the door.

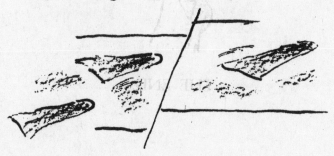

Looby followed them along the landing, down the stairs and through the kitchen to the back door. Outside, the footprints continued down the garden path and away.

The watch-frog *had* managed
to help someone out, she realized.
He'd saved their lives. And the
wicked witch's curse had been
removed.

"Goodbye, watch-frog –
whoever you are," Looby
whispered. "And thank *you!*"

THE END